THE PICNIC

RUTH BROWN

Red Fox

The rabbit sat bolt upright, alert and listening. He had felt the unmistakable rhythm of footsteps – and footsteps meant humans – and humans meant danger!

He knew what to do. He raised the alarm and dived for cover –

underground. The animals waited, listening, tense and rigid, frightened by the dreaded sound of footsteps getting nearer and nearer.

Suddenly it all went black. There was instant darkness.
Total panic and confusion reigned.

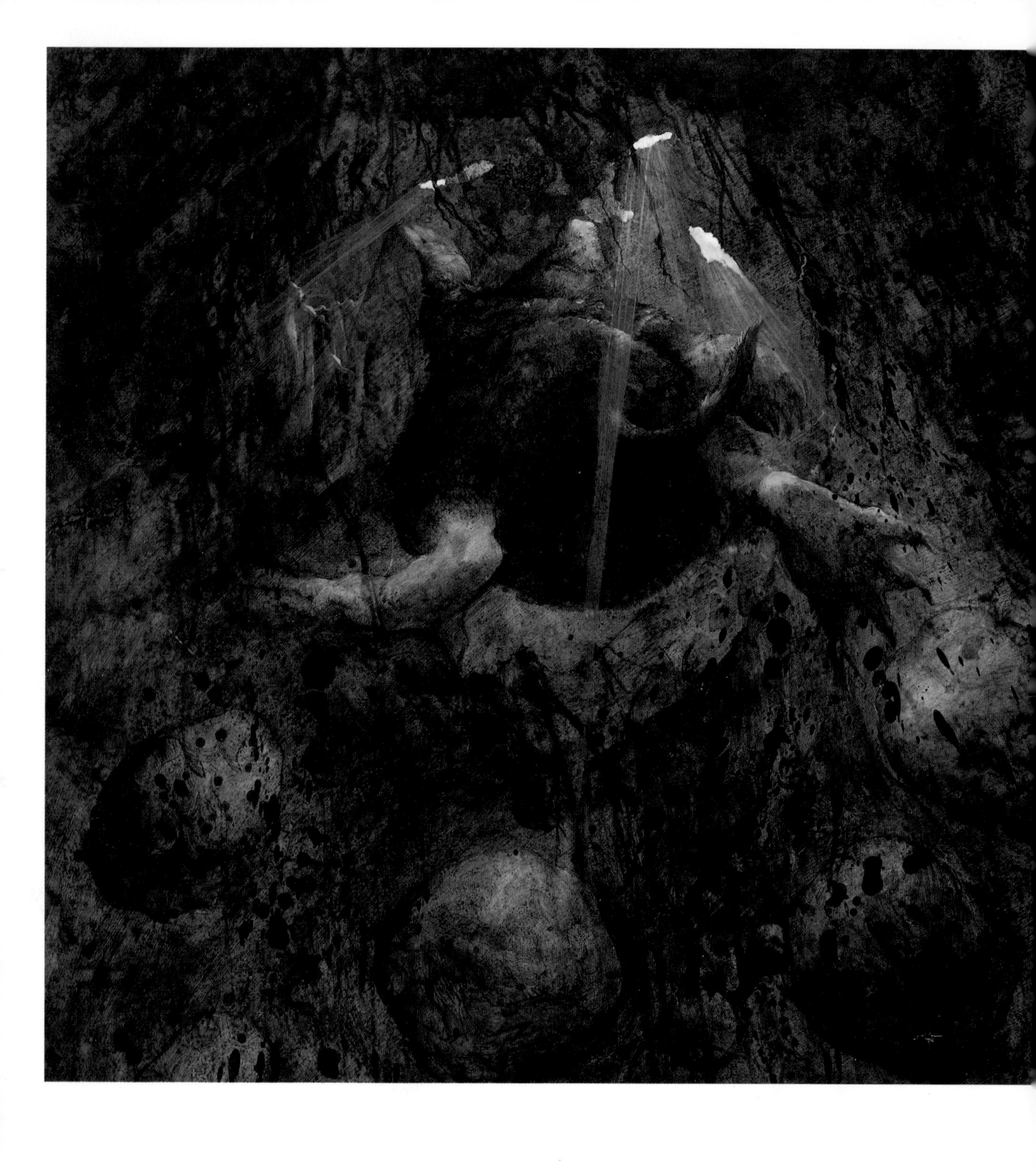

One final heave and he emerged, blinking, into warmth
and light. He couldn't see the danger –

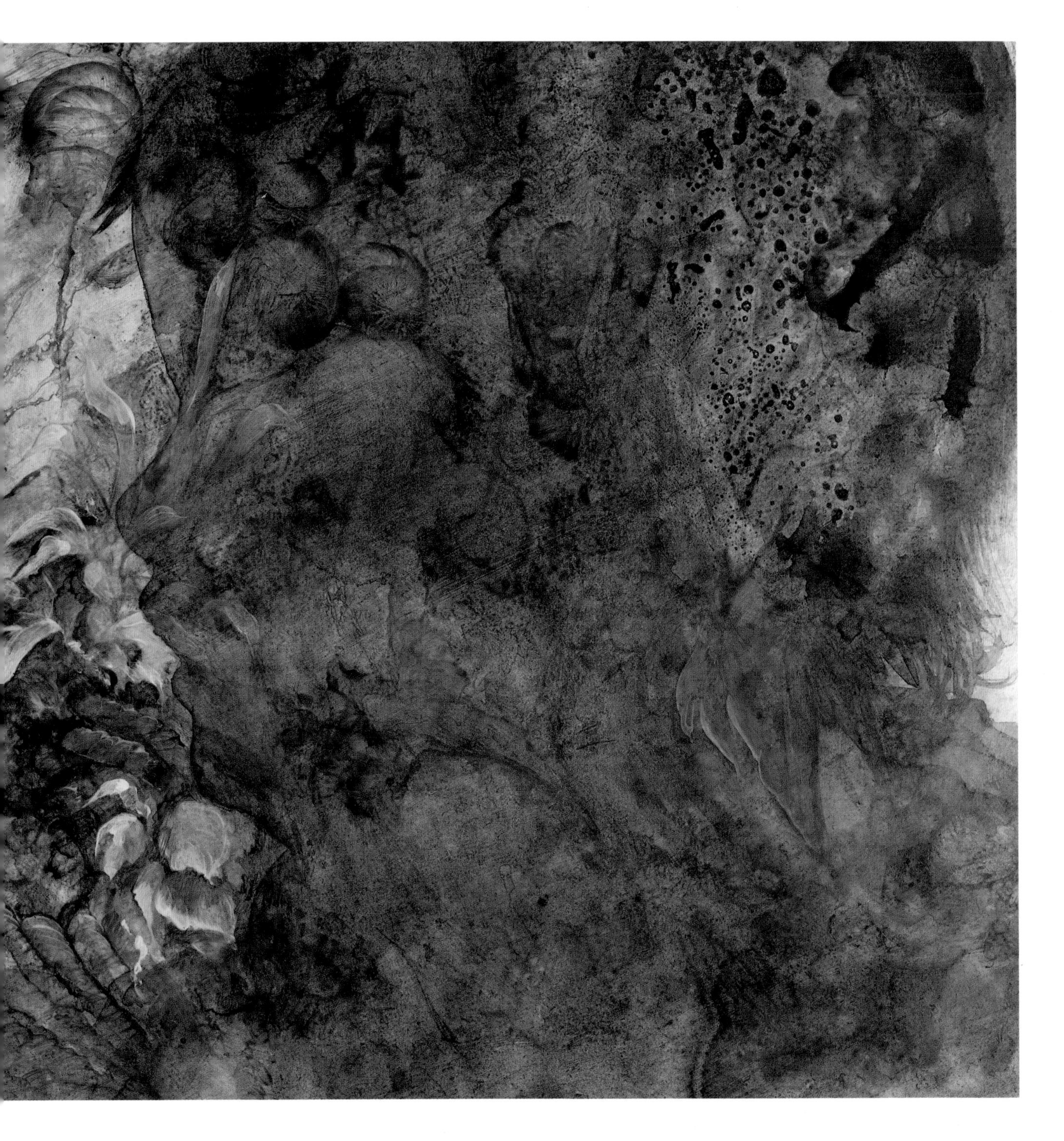

– coming straight towards him –

but Mouse could, and was terrified!

He dragged Mole back down into the darkness, bumping, scraping, bouncing, squealing, dishevelled and undignified, towards the other animals.

But up ahead there was a new danger. Where there should have been daylight, there was a nose –

– and teeth, and scrabbling claws that tore the earth, flinging them in all directions, and worse – water was rushing in. The animals were trapped between the fangs and flood.

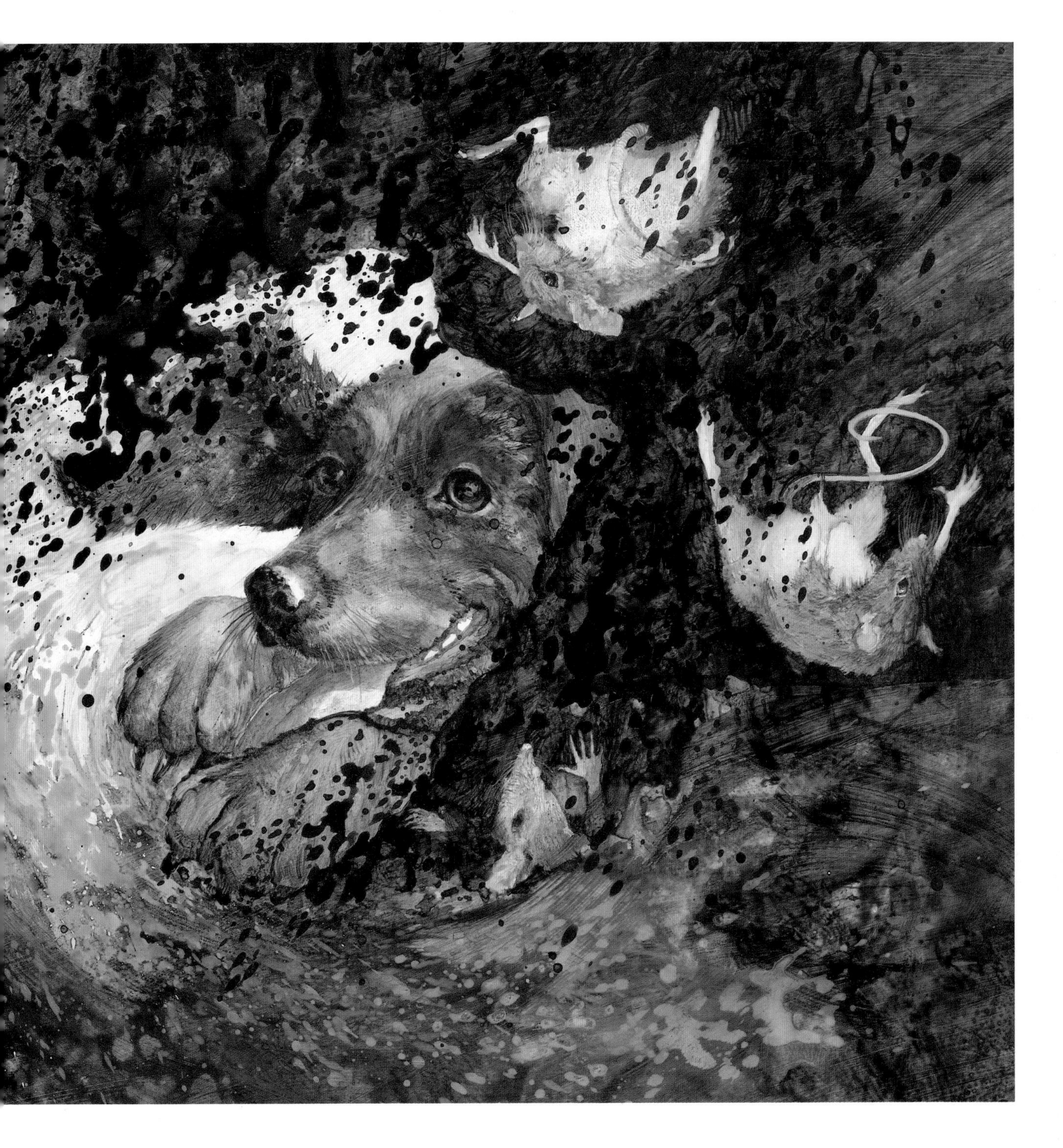

Outside, the dog could chase only one of them; inside, the mud would smother them all.

So, desperately, they scrambled out and found that the dog had fled! Back to his masters, escaping the storm. They stood in the rain and CHEERED!

Later on they had their own picnic with the scraps of food they found. Then after sunset, dry and sleepy, they returned to safety – underground.

A Red Fox Book

Published by Random House Children's Books
20 Vauxhall Bridge Road, London SW1V 2SA

A division of Random House UK Ltd
London Melbourne Sydney Auckland
Johannesburg and agencies throughout the world

First published by Andersen Press Ltd 1992

Red Fox edition 1994

1 3 5 7 9 10 8 6 4 2

Printed in Hong Kong

RANDOM HOUSE UK Limited Reg. No. 954009

ISBN 0 09 929381 1

Some bestselling Red Fox picture books

THE BIG ALFIE AND ANNIE ROSE STORYBOOK
by Shirley Hughes
OLD BEAR
by Jane Hissey
OI! GET OFF OUR TRAIN
by John Burningham
I WANT A CAT
by Tony Ross
NOT NOW, BERNARD
by David McKee
ALL JOIN IN
by Quentin Blake
THE SAND HORSE
by Michael Foreman and Ann Turnbull
BAD BORIS GOES TO SCHOOL
by Susie Jenkin-Pearce
BILBO'S LAST SONG
by J.R.R. Tolkien
MATILDA
by Hilaire Belloc and Posy Simmonds
WILLY AND HUGH
by Anthony Browne
THE WINTER HEDGEHOG
by Ann and Reg Cartwright
A DARK, DARK TALE
by Ruth Brown
HARRY, THE DIRTY DOG
by Gene Zion and Margaret Bloy Graham
DR XARGLE'S BOOK OF EARTHLETS
by Jeanne Willis and Tony Ross
JAKE
by Deborah King